No Frogs
for
Dinner

by Frieda Wishinsky • Illustrated by Linda Hendry

Fitzhenry & Whiteside

First Flight® is a registered trademark of Fitzhenry & Whiteside

Published in Canada by Fitzhenry & Whiteside,
195 Allstate Parkway, Markham, Ontario L3R 4T8

Published in the United States by Fitzhenry & Whiteside,
311 Washington Street, Brighton, Massachusetts 02135

This edition first published by Fitzhenry & Whiteside in 2012

www.fitzhenry.ca   godwit@fitzhenry.ca

10 9 8 7 6 5 4 3 2 1

Library and Archives Canada Cataloguing in Publication
Wishinsky, Frieda
No frogs for dinner / Frieda Wishinsky ; illustrated by Linda Hendry.
ISBN 978-1-55455-189-7
I. Hendry, Linda II. Title.
PS8595.I834N6 2011   jC813'.54   C2011-905865-0

Publisher Cataloging-in-Publication Data (U.S)
Wishinsky, Frieda
No Frogs for Dinner / Frieda Wishinsky ; Linda Hendry.
[ ] p. : col. Ill. ; cm.
Summary: Melvin's trip to the big city is not turning out as he hoped. Instead of hot dogs, baseball and tall buildings, his Aunt Rose drags
him to the opera, museums and fancy restaurants. Melvin must find a way to curb his aunt's enthusiasm long enough to have some real fun.
ISBN: 978-1-5545-5189-7 (pbk.)
1. Adventure – Juvenile fiction. I. Hendry, Linda. II. Title.
[E] dc22 PZ7.W574No   2011

Fitzhenry & Whiteside acknowledges with thanks the Canada Council for the Arts, and the Ontario Arts Council for their support
of our publishing program. We acknowledge the financial support of the Government of Canada through the
Canada Book Fund (CBF) for our publishing activities.

Cover and interior design by Kerry Plumley
Cover image by Linda Hendry
Printed in Hong Kong

For my friend,
Kathy Guttman
F.W.

For Chris and Janet
Who only make "good" things to eat…
L.H.

Melvin couldn't wait to visit the big city.

He'd ride up the
tallest buildings.

He'd go uptown and
downtown by subway.

He'd watch baseball in a giant stadium.

He'd munch pizza and
hot dogs and pretzels.

It would be great!

Finally the day came.

Melvin's parents drove him
to the airport.

"Be a good guest." They said. "Listen to Aunt Rose."

"I will," Melvin promised.

The plane rose in the sky.

Soon Melvin saw fluffy clouds.

Soon Melvin saw long bridges.

Soon Melvin saw the city!

With a bounce the plane landed and Melvin stepped out.

"Melvin! Melvin!" called Aunt Rose.

She scooped him into her arms.

She squeezed him like a tomato.

"Hurry!" she said. "I've planned EVERYTHING!"

"Everything?" said Melvin, as they leaped into a cab.

"First the Museum of Natural History!" said Aunt Rose.

They headed for the dinosaurs
immediately.

Aunt Rose asked Melvin what
the Tyrannosaurus ate.

She asked him what the Stegosaurus drank.

She asked him how tall, how fat, how long, how fast the Brontosaurus was.

But Melvin couldn't answer.

Aunt Rose answered for him.

"Now for the Museum of Modern Art," said Aunt Rose.

Aunt Rose zipped him past strange paintings and sculptures.

She talked about artists, colors and shapes.

She talked and talked and talked.

Finally she stopped talking and whisked him into a cab.

The cab zigzagged and zoomed.

"Where are we going?" asked Melvin.

"Shopping!" sang Aunt Rose.

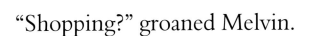

"Shopping?" groaned Melvin.

"First a tie for your dad," said Aunt Rose.

"Dad hates ties," said Melvin.

"He'll love this one," said Aunt Rose.

"Now a scarf for your mom," said Aunt Rose.

"Mom doesn't wear scarves," said Melvin.

"She'll wear this one!" said Aunt Rose.

"Now for you!"

"I don't want anything," said Melvin.

"Pish posh," said Aunt Rose.

Aunt Rose picked out a tee shirt for Melvin.

"Try it on!" said Aunt Rose.

"I'd rather not," said Melvin.

"For me," said Aunt Rose.

Melvin tried on the tee shirt.

Aunt Rose pinched his cheek.

"You look adorable. We'll buy two!

Now for sushi."

"What's sushi?" asked Melvin.

"Raw fish wrapped in fish skins and seaweed."

Melvin ate two bowls of rice.

"Time for the opera!" sang Aunt Rose.

"I'm a little tired," said Melvin.

"The opera will perk you up," said Aunt Rose.

18

At the opera, the singers sang

and sang

and sang.

By Act Two Melvin
was sound asleep.

"Poor darling," said Aunt Rose on the way home.

"Right to bed. Tomorrow is a busy day."

Aunt Rose woke him at seven.

She made oatmeal, stewed prunes and tea.

"How about a nice poached egg?" she suggested.

"I'm stuffed," said Melvin.

"Don't worry," said Aunt Rose.

"You'll walk it off at the Botanical Gardens."

22

Aunt Rose dragged him from flower to flower.

"Smell this," she said.

"Smell that."

Melvin smelled hundreds of flowers.

"Now, oysters for lunch!" announced Aunt Rose.

"How do you eat oysters?" asked Melvin.

"You open your mouth and they slide down," said Aunt Rose.

Melvin gulped.

"Aunt Rose," he began, "I…I…"

"You want to know about dinner. We're having frogs' legs."

"What?" Melvin gasped.

"Frogs, darling, frogs!" sang Aunt Rose.

Melvin stared at Aunt Rose.

He couldn't.

He wouldn't.

"No," he said.

"What?" gasped Aunt Rose.

"NO. I'm not eating frogs."
Melvin said.

"No, I'm not eating oysters…

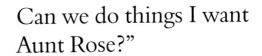

Can we do things I want
Aunt Rose?"

Aunt Rose stared at Melvin.

"Why, Melvin, darling, why
didn't you tell me?

You should always speak up."

"I am," said Melvin.

"I want to ride up the tallest skyscraper.

I want to go uptown and downtown by subway.

I want to watch baseball in a giant stadium.

I want…"

"Stop, Melvin!" said Aunt Rose.

"My head is spinning."

"But can we? Can we?"
asked Melvin.

"Of course we can, darling," said Aunt Rose.

"After all, Melvin, you're my guest!"

And Melvin was!